JAMILA GAVIN

The Magic Orange Tree

and other stories

Illustrated by Ossie Murray

mammoth

First published in Great Britain 1979
by Methuen Children's Books Ltd
Published 2000 by Mammoth
an imprint of Egmont Children's Books Limited,
a division of Egmont Holding Limited
239 Kensington High Street, London W8 6SA

ISBN 0 7497 2201 0

10 9 8 7 6 5 4 3 2 1

A CIP catalogue record for this title
is available from the British Library

Printed in Great Britain
by Cox & Wyman Ltd, Reading, Berkshire

Contents

Introduction

The children in these stories live in a city, but in their fantasies they can be anywhere and anything might happen.

They have adventures on moonlit nights when cats stalk and cows meander; they fly through the air on the backs of dragons or clutched in the claws of a giant bird.

They play in alleys and on street corners; round tower blocks and housing estates; they creep in and out of gardens and churchyards; their hiding places and dens are where the shrubs become the jungle, and dusty backyards the back of the moon.

Sometimes the children meet in the park. They play the same games and talk about the same things – and yet they are different from each other. Some of their mothers and fathers come from far-off countries to make their homes in this city. They come from Africa and Asia; from Poland and Cyprus – or just from other parts of Britain. They eat different food and some wear strange clothes — but they all have stories to tell. Whenever their parents, grandparents or aunts and uncles meet there is always a lot of talk about memories of distant places. The children listen and remember: they hear of warm nights and orange trees, of dragon dances and long journeys, of parties and music and friendliness.

These memories and stories become part of the children's dreams; part of their make-believe. They play in the city, but in their fantasies they can go anywhere.

Pearly's adventure with the giant bird

It had rained all morning. When it stopped, Ma said to her children, 'Come on, Pearly and Winston, get yourselves ready, we are going visiting.'

'Oh must we?' groaned the children. They hated visiting.

'Yes, you must – and that's final. We are having tea with Aunt Josie and Uncle Charlie. Winston! Go wake up your Pa.' Pa was slumped in an armchair snoring quietly behind a Sunday paper.

'Pearly! I want you to wear your new dress. Aunt Josie hasn't seen it yet.'

That was a treat. Pearly loved her new dress. It was blue georgette, spangled with silver thread; there were frills round the sleeves and bottom, and tons of white net petticoat that made the skirt stick out; round her middle was a broad sash which tied at the back in a bow. It was a beautiful dress – her Ma had made it! She made all

Pearly's clothes. When she was dressed, Ma did Pearly's hair. She skilfully brushed it up into neat little tufts all over her head – just as her own hair had been done when she was a little girl back home in Ghana.

Winston had to wear his long, black trousers and striped shirt with a bow tie to match. When he was dressed up – all smart like that – he looked just like his Pa.

The pavements were still damp when they finally set off. The sky was grey and the streets looked dull. But it was not cold, and Pearly did not have to hide her pretty dress under a coat. Pa walked in front – straight and upright – whirling his umbrella. Ma followed just a shoulder behind, trying to hurry the children along when they dawdled. Pearly and Winston hopped along the pavement making sure that they only trod in the squares. If you trod on a line you plunged down a ravine! Suddenly Winston saw something in the sky. He stopped and tugged Pearly's arm. 'What's that, Pearly?' he asked in a puzzled voice.

'I don't know,' said Pearly frowning.

'Perhaps it's Concorde,' said Winston

excitedly. He had always wanted to see Con-corde.

'It can't be!' said Pearly scornfully, 'it's not making any noise.'

'Is it a dragon, then?' asked Winston, a little more drastically.

'No, silly!' replied Pearly. But she did not sound so confident now. What was it?

The children both stood stock still star-ing, as the 'thing' came nearer and nearer.

'Ma!' shouted the children.

'Don't dawdle,' said Ma without looking back.

'Come along! Come along!' urged Pa, waving his umbrella.

'It's a bird, Pearly!' whispered Winston. 'A giant bird!'

Suddenly the bird seemed to gather speed, then it swooped down, aiming straight for Pearly. Before Pearly could even cry out, the great bird had snatched her up in his talons – and she found herself air-borne.

'Hey! That's my sister!' cried Winston. 'Put her down!'

But the bird only flapped his powerful wings and rose higher and higher.

'Ma! Pa!' yelled Winston. 'Help!'

Mother and father turned round. 'Winston, why can't you walk without always fooling about?' said father sternly.

'Where's Pearly?' asked Ma.

'That's what I was trying to tell you,' said Winston. 'She's been carried off by a giant bird!'

Mother and father stared up at the sky. They could see a speck, but it was so far away that they could not be sure what it was.

'It could be a hot-air balloon,' said Pa.

'It's Pearly,' insisted Winston.

'The colour is the same as her dress,' agreed Ma . . .'Ohhhh . . . Pearly . . . is that really her?' she wailed.

'Stuff and nonsense!' retorted Pa. 'Come on, let's get on to Aunt Josie and Uncle Charlie. Perhaps Pearly has played a trick on us and gone on ahead.'

But Pearly was not there. 'I tell you, Pearly got carried off by a giant bird.' said Winston stubbornly.

Meanwhile, Pearly dangled from the giant bird's claws. The bird flew over the new super-market and block of flats; over the town hall in the town centre; he

14

skimmed past the war memorial in the municipal gardens, and flew on to the hill in the middle of the park. At the top of the hill, at the top of the tallest tree, the bird had built a nest. There he dropped Pearly with a plop – right in the middle, and then he flew off squawking loudly.

Pearly sulked. This was not her day. It was bad enough having to go visiting, but to be captured by a giant bird, carried off like some rag doll, then dumped in a nest at the top of the tallest tree – and in her best dress too – was more than she could bear. She began to wail. She looked out of the nest to see if there was any way down, but when she saw how high she was she just felt dizzy. Then she began to yell . . . 'Help! Help! . . .' but her voice got carried away on the wind.

After a while, the giant bird returned. It was carrying a huge, juicy worm in its beak. Pearly screamed. 'Don't you dare drop that on me!'

The bird was so surprised that he swallowed the worm himself. 'That was supposed to be your supper,' he said with a gulp.

'I don't eat worms!' grumbled Pearly. 'Anyway, why did you carry me off?'

'I made a mistake,' said the bird. 'I thought you were an interesting item. I collect interesting items – haven't you noticed all my fascinating objects of art and exquisite curios?'

Pearly looked around her. The nest was full of the most interesting things indeed; rings that sparkled; beads that glittered; and entwined in and out of the leaves and twigs that made up the nest were all sorts of ribbons of satin and silk which flashed and shone.

'I was flying over the town,' explained the giant bird, 'looking for more interesting items for my collection. At first I thought, "What a dull town." The sky was so grey and all the colours looked bleak and miserable. Then suddenly your blue dress caught my eye; the silver-spangled threads sparkled even on such a day; it was irresistible. I'm afraid all I could think about was picking it up to bring to my nest. I did not even stop to think someone might be inside the dress. So sorry.' He ended apologetically.

'That's all right,' said Pearly – not so cross

now. 'I understand. It is a beautiful dress. My mother made it. She makes all my dresses. I could give you lots of pretty cloth for your collection – but how am I going to get home?'

'That's easy!' said the bird. 'I'll take you back. You're as light as a feather! But please, please, before you go, could I have a scrap of blue, silver-spangled georgette from your dress?'

'Of course you can!' said Pearly. 'You can have the sash.' She undid the enormous bow and pulled off the long, flowing sash. The giant bird was so delighted he began to sing an amazing song. He picked up the sash in his beak and whisked it about, watching it flash and sparkle. He warbled and whistled so happily that Pearly clapped her hands and laughed with joy. She didn't feel sulky any more. This was much better than visiting!

Then the giant bird picked Pearly gently up in his talons and flew out of the nest. Pearly told the bird that he had better take her to Uncle Charlie's house – 'That's where my folks will be,' she said. So the bird flew and flew, back over the park; over the war memorial and the town hall; and over the block of flats and the new super-market.

'There's Uncle Charlie and Aunt Josie's house!' cried Pearly, 'and oh look! There's my brother Winston outside the house. Winston!' she called.

The giant bird dropped lower and lower. Then just at the top of the street he hovered a few inches from the ground. Pearly landed gently on her feet.

'Goodbye, bird!' she called. 'I'll come and visit you in the park with lots more interesting items for your collection.'

'Thank you,' replied the bird, 'but I think your beautiful sash will always be my pride and joy.' Then with a wonderful whistle and warble he flew away.

When Winston saw his sister he came running. 'Pearly! Pearly! Where have you been? Ma and Pa are hopping mad.'

'I got carried off by a giant bird, you saw me,' said Pearly.

'That's what I kept telling them,' said Winston, 'but I don't think they believed me.'

Pearly and Winston went inside. There were Ma, Pa, Uncle Charlie and Aunt Josie.

'Where have you been?' thundered Pa.

'Where is the sash from your dress?' wailed Ma.

'Pearly! You've been a worry to your mother,' said Uncle Charlie sternly.

'What have you been up to in your beautiful new dress?' exclaimed Aunt Josie.

'I got carried off by a giant bird!' said Pearly.

Everyone stood with their mouths open. No one said a word. Well, there was nothing anyone could say, was there?

Robbie and the fearsome beastie

Robbie loved thinking about monsters. He imagined them everywhere. In the coal bunkers, under the stairs or in the water-pipes. At night he was not sure if there was a monster hiding under his bed, so he would take a running jump and land with a plop in the middle of the bed, just in case a long hairy arm was waiting to grab his ankle.

At the bottom of the garden, on the other side of the fence, was a canal. Robbie knew that the biggest and most dangerous monster of all lived in that brown, murky water. If he climbed on to the garden shed, he could see all sorts of things drift slowly by; bits of wood, an old tyre or bundles of rags. Sometimes the sun would flash on the water; something would ripple the surface, and Robbie would stare and stare, certain it was a monster moving about down there.

Once they had gone to Scotland for a holiday to stay with old Grandpa MacPherson. He had told Robbie all about the Loch Ness Monster. ' "Loch" is the Scottish word for "lake",' explained Grandfather. 'Loch Ness is very, very deep and dangerous. People say a fearsome beastie lives in the lake. Many say that they have caught a glimpse of it, and others that they have taken photographs. But no one has seen it for long enough or often enough for everyone to believe it. Even when a submarine went down to have a look, they were not absolutely sure that they saw her – it was too dark and gloomy.

People see her by accident. Sometimes they are walking or sitting by the lake, when suddenly they see a hump – or even two or three humps; or they see a serpent-like head speeding through the water leaving a trail of ripples behind. They only have time to shout, "Hey, did you see that!" then it is gone. Your dad, when he was a wee laddie, he used to go looking for the Loch Ness Monster.'

'Do you think there is a monster in our canal back home?' Robbie had asked excitedly.

'Maybe there is and maybe there isn't,'

Grandfather had replied mysteriously. 'You will just have to keep watching.'

So Robbie did keep watching. When they got home again, the first thing he did was to climb on top of the garden shed and look so hard down into the depths of the canal that his eyes watered. He longed to see the flick of a tail or the tip of a hump, but he only saw the flies skimming the surface with their wings, and leaves floating by like little boats.

When Grandpa MacPherson came from Scotland to stay with them for a holiday, Robbie took him for walks along the canal. When he was young, Grandfather used to work on a barge on the canals. In fact he had seen most of England and Scotland from his boat. Now the canals were not in use. All the goods were carried by road and rail, but Grandfather still loved the canals.

'Are you still looking for that fearsome beastie, Robbie?' asked Grandpa.

'Yes,' said Robbie, 'and I'm sure that one lives in this canal. Not as big or important as the one in Loch Ness, but very, very dangerous.'

'I'll help you keep a lookout,' said

Grandpa, 'but if your monster has any sense he will stay hidden. He must know that if anyone sees him it will be the end of his peace and quiet. That one in Loch Ness must already be plagued with monster-spotters. Tourists come tramping up and down the shore looking for tracks; sailing all over the lake in boats and steamers; gaping through binoculars. And if they did see him? What then? Can you imagine it, Robbie, television cameras would be all over the place; directors from zoos; collectors, speculators, zoologists, biologists – every kind of ologist from John O'Groats to Timbuktu. Look you here, laddie, if ever you do see the monster who lives in this canal, don't you ever say a word to anyone, will you now?' the old man said passionately.

'No, Grandpa,' said Robbie firmly, 'I won't.'

Down on the slimy bottom of the canal, the monster rested. His long, long body wound endlessly along the narrow water-way. Suddenly, the water heaved; a tail lashed to and fro, flicking the grasses and weeds that grew on each bank. A head broke through the surface and rose higher and higher on the end of a long neck; for a moment it swivelled round, gazing at the brick houses, yards and gardens which backed on to his domain. Then like an amazing switchback he looped and swooped down the length of the canal. He seemed to play; first racing between the narrow lines of the bank; then diving so fiercely, that the water became a whirlpool, sucking in the debris. He lunged and rolled so that mighty waves swamped the tow paths.

Robbie came out to play. The monster glided like a serpent down to the bottom. As the mud settled over his cold body, the furious waters gradually calmed. Robbie climbed on to the garden shed. He frowned as he looked at the last ripples rolling down the canal. He noticed the flattened grasses and the sodden path. There was a lunch-time stillness. Even the quarrelsome sparrows were hushed. Robert watched and waited.

The monster had a problem. He was growing. The canal had been a good home for him as a young monster, but suddenly he had begun to get bigger and bigger. It would not be long before some of his humps would stick up above the water. He knew that he would grow bigger than a house and as long as a street. He had to find a new home. But he could not just heave himself up out of his canal and go stumping through the town looking for a more suitable home. He needed help. So at the same time as Robbie and Grandpa were looking out for the monster, the monster often wallowed just under the grimy surface looking at them. He watched and waited.

Grandpa came out after his afternoon nap. 'Hullo, Robbie,' he called, 'any sign of the beastie yet?'

'I haven't exactly seen him,' replied Robbie thoughtfully, 'but I'm sure he's been up and about today. Have you noticed how flat the grass is and look at the tow path – it's been swamped. It's all muddy.'

'Och away,' Grandpa said as he bent down to look closer at the banks and the path. 'Gracious!' he breathed. He pottered up and down, prodding with his stick and gazing into the canal. At last he stopped and pulled out his pipe. He gave a puff or two. 'Gracious!' he said again.

'Grandpa!' called Robbie in an excited

voice, 'can you see a kind of bubble in the water over there? It looks a bit like an eye. It seems to be looking at us!'

'It's probably a toad,' said Grandpa, 'they have bubbly eyes.' Then all of a sudden he saw what Robbie meant. It did seem to be an eye – but not a toad's eye. This was the size of a dinner plate! As they stared in disbelief, the eye blinked. Then the whole of the monster's huge body gradually rose to the surface so that they could see all of him.

'Gracious!' exclaimed Grandpa and Robbie together.

The monster stretched away as far as they could see; his tail disappeared round the bend. His body broadened in the middle and he could rest his flippers on each bank. He raised his head up . . . up . . . up . . . until he could see into the upstairs windows. Then, when he had shown them how big he was, he slowly submerged himself and sank beneath the churning water. Only his eye – as big as a dinner plate – gazed at them from the middle of the canal.

'He's too big for this canal!' cried Robbie. 'It must be an awful squash!'

'That's it, Robbie my boy, that's it. That

must be what he was trying to tell us. He wants us to find him a new home!' Grandpa jumped up and down waving his stick.

'Where can he go?' asked Robbie.

'Let's think,' replied Grandfather.

'The swimming baths?'

'No, not big enough – and anyway, too noisy.'

'The boating pond in the park?'

'No, he'd upset the boats.'

'I wish we could take him to Loch Ness,' said Robbie, 'he'd have plenty of room, and a friend for company.' Then he said, 'What about the gravel pits?'

'The gravel pits! That's it – and they are only a short walk from the canal side. Good, Robbie, that's a grand idea,' said Grandpa enthusiastically. 'We must make the beastie swim along under the railway bridge, past the factory until he's at the waste ground. From there he can walk across to the gravel pits.'

'I hope he'll follow us,' said Robbie.

'I'm sure he will,' said Grandfather.

'What are you two cooking?' came a voice. It was Robbie's Mum.

'Robbie and I have to get a friend out of trouble,' said Grandfather.

'Who is your friend?' asked mother.

Robbie and Grandpa looked at each other, 'Shall we tell?' They nodded.

'It's just the monster who lives in the canal,' said Robbie, 'he's grown too big for it, so we are going to help him move to the gravel pits.'

She laughed. 'Well, be sure to be back for tea – the pair of you – I'm just about to pop some scones into the oven.' She went off shaking her head – 'Monsters indeed!'

It was a Saturday afternoon. Most of the town was at a football match or watching it on television. Grandpa thought it was a good time to make the move. He and Robbie stood on the edge of the canal looking for some sign of the monster. The water stirred slightly and suddenly they saw the bubbly eye peering at them. Grandpa waved his stick, then he and Robbie began to walk slowly towards the railway bridge.

'Is he following?' whispered Robbie.

'I don't know. He's staying hidden,' replied Grandpa. 'Keep walking.'

They walked under the railway bridge

and past the factory. They could hear the roars and chants from the football stadium. As they neared the gravel pits, the houses ended and there was a lot of waste ground.

'This is the tricky bit,' said Grandpa, 'I hope he has not forgotten how to walk.'

They found a track and began to follow it. They walked a few paces and turned round. There was no sign of him. They walked further. Then Robbie looked round. 'Grandpa,' he shrieked, 'he's coming!'

The monster had heaved himself out of the canal and was following. His stubby legs had to carry the huge, dripping body; he staggered awkwardly, his neck stretched far out in front, and his tail trailing miles behind. He swayed this way and that, flapping his flippers to keep his balance. It was an amazing sight.

At last they reached the edge of the gravel pits. A chilly wind ruffled the grey surface. Robbie and Grandpa stood well back as the monster lurched nearer and nearer. When at last he arrived, he looked round at Robbie and Grandpa, then raising his head he gave a shuddering sigh. A flock of gulls rose in terror from the water. Then he gathered himself together and dived into the water. His huge body disappeared with barely a splash.

'He's gone,' said Robbie sadly.

'Yes, he's gone, but he'll never forget you,' said Grandpa.

Robbie and Grandpa went silently back home for tea. The smell of his Mum's scones made them feel hungry.

'Did the move go all right?' asked Mum.

'Oh yes, very well,' replied Grandpa. 'I don't think that beastie will need to move for another couple of hundred years.'

'I wish he hadn't had to go,' said Robbie. 'I liked having a monster at the bottom of my garden.'

Aziz and the amazing motorbike ride

Aziz sat in his wheelchair looking out of the window.

In each long day it was the afternoons that seemed the longest part. He would wait and wait, watching for the moment when the children would explode out of school. That was the best time.

But now he just gazed out of the window at other people's back gardens. He could see Mrs Lal hanging out her saris on the washing line; Mr Yates digging his garden, and over there was Masood – tinkering with his motorbike.

Aziz loved that motorbike. He wanted to see Masood jump on the starter and hear the engine catch and turn over. He wanted to hear him open up the throttle and rev up until a great roar filled the neighbourhood. He knew this made Mrs Lal very angry because it woke her baby. She would shake her fist and hold her head. Mr Yates did not like it much either and he would yell at Masood and tell him to be quiet. But Aziz thought the noise of the motorbike was the greatest sound in the world. Whenever he heard it he would push himself up in his chair until his arms were straight – as if the power of the machine could lift him out of his chair.

This afternoon Masood did not look as if he were going to take the bike out. He lay on his back with an oil can at his side, greasing the engine and cleaning the parts. When the job was done he went back indoors to wash. Aziz flopped back, disappointed. The motorbike stood proudly on its stand, its chrome and paintwork gleaming in the sunlight.

Suddenly Aziz heard the kick of the starter and the roar of the engine. He looked up – but too late! The motorbike had gone.

'Oh no! I missed him!' groaned Aziz. 'Masood must have come out so quickly.' He listened to the sound of the engine as it went down the alley that ran between the gardens. But strangely enough, the sound seemed very close. Right next to him! Aziz leaned forward to look out and gave a shout of excitement. There at his window – with the engine running – stood the motorbike!

'Come for a ride,' said the motorbike. 'I'm shiny and oiled and full of petrol.'

'How can I?' cried Aziz. 'Since my accident I cannot move my legs.'

'Just slide on to my seat,' said the motorbike. 'Grip my handle-bars and I'll do the rest.'

So Aziz stretched out as far as he could and seemed to float through the window. In a second he was astride the motorbike. Masood's helmet and goggles were hanging from the handle-bars. Aziz put them on and felt like a motorcycle champion.

'I'm ready!' he shouted.

'RRRRrrrmmmm . . . RRRRrrrmmmm . . . RRRrrrmmm . . . RRRrrrmmm . . . the motorbike roared. Aziz felt the power rush through him – and then they were off.

They flashed down the alley and out on to the main road. Cars and lorries whizzed past them on each side. The motorbike revved and accelerated into the traffic. Aziz leaned with the machine as it darted in and out, and turned corners so sharply – that

Aziz thought he would brush the road with the handle-bars.

They joined a motorway and soon left the city far behind. As they streaked across the countryside, Aziz felt as if they were having a race with the wind.

'There's a fair going on over there!' cried the motorbike. 'Would you like to see it?'

'Oh yes! replied Aziz excitedly.

They followed the sound of music blasting out over a loudspeaker and soon found the fair in a field.

People were milling about in and out of tents and stalls. Some tried their luck throwing hoops, or fishing for gifts; others tested their aim on the rifle range.

Aziz and the motorbike weaved their way between the ice-cream sellers and the hot-dog vans. Over on the other side was the main attraction – 'STEVE SPEED – THE WORLD FAMOUS STUNT MOTOR-CYCLIST'.

They joined the crowd pressing round the enclosure. Steve Speed came racing in at about sixty miles an hour. He thundered up a ramp and jumped over six barrels; he did it again and jumped over ten barrels!

36

Everyone cheered. Now there was a wall of fire. Steve Speed drove round the field and accelerated towards the flames. Aziz hid his eyes as he disappeared into the fire; but a split second later he was out the other side – waving and unharmed. Then he went on to do daring acrobatics. He stood on his hands; lay down as if his machine were a bed; he jumped on and off and even let the motorbike run away from him – only to leap back on again as it circled round. Aziz was thrilled.

'I think it's time we showed them a trick or two!' said Masood's motorbike. 'Hold tight!' They roared into the ring. The crowd was cheering. They flashed round the field then suddenly tipped up on to the back wheel and circled on just one wheel! The motorbike spun like a top and bounced like a ball; someone brought out a flaming hoop.

'Put your head down!' yelled the motorbike. Then it zoomed up the ramp. The crowd held its breath as the machine shot like a thunderbolt – bull's-eye – right through the hoop of flames.

On the far side of the field was a car park. 'This is our last trick,' said the motorbike.

'Are you still holding tight?' Aziz gripped the handle-bars; the motorbike revved and revved; the pitch rose until it sounded like an aeroplane.

'What are they going to do now?' asked a hushed voice from the crowd. Aziz and the motorbike held back for a moment as everything throbbed. Then they shot forwards up the ramp and exploded like a rocket straight over the top. They flew through the air . . . on and on . . . and on . . . The crowd could not believe its eyes. They flew right over the cars and coaches in the car park . . . over the fences and hedges . . . and finally made a perfect landing in the road on the other side.

As they turned towards home, Aziz could hear the crowds clapping and cheering wildly. 'They have never seen a trick as good as that before – not even from Steve Speed,' said Aziz proudly.

They sped back along the motorway. It was nearly four o'clock. As they reached the High Street, school doors were flung open and children came tumbling out.

Aziz saw his friends and waved. 'David! Jimmy!' he called, 'look at me!' But they did not seem to see him.

'They don't recognise me,' said Aziz. 'It must be the helmet and goggles. Never mind, I'll tell them all about it when they come and see me.'

The motorbike turned down the narrow alleyway. When it reached Aziz's house it stopped outside his window.

'Thanks for the wonderful ride,' sighed Aziz happily.

'RRRRmmmm . . . RRRRmmmm . . .' replied the motorbike.

Aziz took off the helmet and goggles and hung them as before on the handle-bars. Then he reached up and seemed to float back into his room.

Once more in his wheelchair, Aziz leaned back still panting. His cheeks were rosy with excitement. His mother came in with some tea.

'Hello, Aziz,' she said. 'You look pleased about something. Have you just been to the moon?'

Aziz laughed. 'No, Mother! I've only been for a ride on that motorbike.'

They both looked across to Masood's garden where the motorbike stood polished and glinting – just waiting to be off!

How Grandma saved the day

Today was the day. The day that Maria was seven years old, and the day of her party. Her mother and grandmother had been busy all morning making triangle sandwiches, moulding jellies and putting the icing on the cake. Dad came home from work early to blow up balloons.

'We are going to splash out this year and have an entertainer to run the party,' Dad had said. So Mum sighed, 'Thank heavens!' and concentrated on the food instead of organising games.

Yes – Mr Smiley and his incredible bag of tricks, not to mention his famous puppet, Archibald, were going to be the life and soul of the party.

Maria peeped into the kitchen. Her little, black grandmother was bending over and popping a tray of sausage rolls into the oven. Maria called her 'Little Black Grandmother' because she was always dressed from head to toe in black.

'It is the custom where I come from,' said Grandmother.

Grandmother had come from Cyprus to live with them after Grandfather died. At first she was quiet and rather sad. She did not speak English and was afraid to go out. But gradually Maria won her over. 'Play with me, Grandma,' she would say. Grandma would play with her. Not just quiet grandma-ish games, but hilarious, mischievous games; chasing and hiding, or witches and wizards. Sometimes her mother got cross and told Grandmother off.

'You over-excite the child,' she would say, then grumble on in Greek so that Maria did not understand.

Grandma loved singing and dancing.

'Your grandfather was a wonderful dancer!' she told Maria.

'Show me! Show me!' begged Maria.

Then Grandma would stretch out her arms and click her fingers, her head would turn this way and that as she stamped her feet and began to turn, singing loudly as she went. Sometimes the dance would get quicker and quicker. Maria would join in and the two would go whirling round the room clicking and stamping. Then mother would rush in.

'Do you want to get us thrown out?' she would cry.

It's true they lived in a block of flats with people above and below.

'Oh dear!' sighed Grandma, 'England difficult place to live.'

Today, Grandma was keeping strictly to the kitchen. She pottered quietly about like a fairy, making an ordinary plate of sandwiches look magical as she decorated it; a wedge of tomato here, a sprig of parsley there.

'Your guests will be here soon, dear,' called her mother.

Maria looked at herself in the mirror. Did she look older? She felt older from the minute she had woken up. She twirled round in her party dress and decided that she definitely looked seven and not six.

'When is Mr Smiley coming?' called mother.

'He should be here now,' replied Father. The door-bell rang. 'That will be him.'

It wasn't. It was the first guest.

Maria stood near the door to greet her

friends as they now began to arrive, one after the other.

Soon five little boys and five little girls were helping Maria to tear the wrapping off her presents. Soon five little boys and five little girls were looking for amusement.

'Where *is* Mr Smiley?' hissed mother.

'I don't know, dear,' moaned Father.

The children trooped through the flat. Dad tried to take charge and scattered balloons.

'Where's the tea?' called a child.

'Not yet, not yet!' said Mother. 'In half an hour.'

But what will they do for half an hour? Where was Mr Smiley and his incredible bag of tricks – not to mention his famous puppet, Archibald? Dad said, 'Let's play Blind Man's Buff.' The telephone rang. Dad answered.

'Hullo! This is Mr Smiley speaking. I am very sorry but my car has broken down. I'm afraid I'm not going to be able to get to the party. I'm waiting for the breakdown service – but you know how long they can be!'

Dad went to the kitchen and broke the news.

43

'I knew I should have organised some games,' wept Mother. 'I haven't even got a "Pass the Parcel" ready.'

The five little boys and five little girls were beginning to sound like five hundred elephants!

Suddenly Little Black Grandmother said, 'I go!' She washed her hands and pattered out of the kitchen. Mother and Father waited. What could Little Black Grandmother, who barely spoke English, do with ten rioting children?

To their amazement the noise stopped. Suddenly they heard other noises – the sound of tapping and clapping; shaking and rattling. Mother and Father peeped round the door. Maria and her friends were sitting on the floor while standing up on the best, polished, mahogany table stood little black grandmother! Mother nearly called out 'STOP!' But Father held her back.

'SSssh – Let her do it!'

Grandma held out her black skirts. She began to sing and tap her foot. She twisted this way and that and beckoned the children to accompany her. She had found them all something to shake or rattle; boxes of pins

44

or buttons; a tin of rice; some old spoons and pieces of corrugated cardboard.

The song got louder and faster. Grandma began to spin and stamp. The children shook and banged and clicked with all their might. Then Grandma jumped down from the table crying, 'Dance, children, dance!'

'What about the neighbours?' wailed Mother.

'They know there is a party going on,' said Dad. 'Come on – I'm joining in!'

Soon Dad, Mum, Grandma, Maria and all her friends had linked arms and were swaying to and fro. They formed a circle and moved inwards and outwards, picking up the tune as Grandma sang.

By tea-time they were starving. They sat round the table in their party hats and for a few moments there was a hush as the sandwiches vanished; then the sausage rolls and the jellies.

'Dancing makes you hungry,' muttered a child with his mouth full.

Then Mother carried in the birthday cake. Everybody gasped. It was pink and white with a ballerina poised in the middle, and seven candles burning brightly. Maria blew out the candles and wished. Her wish was a secret of course!

After tea the children called for Little, Black Grandmother to entertain them – and she did. It was the best party ever known in Belvedere Flats. When the mothers and fathers came to collect their children, they found Little Black Grandmother surrounded by ten, hot-faced, happy children listening enthralled to a story about a sea monster who ate beautiful maidens – not minding that half the words were in Greek!

The next day the neighbours said, 'That was a fine party you had, Maria! It was fun having Mr Smiley then! It pays to get in a good entertainer.'

'That wasn't Mr Smiley,' laughed Maria. 'He never came. That was my lovely, Little Black Grandmother. It was thanks to her.'

The neighbours looked at Maria's grandmother – with whom they had never spoken a word – and were amazed.

'Well I never!' they said, as Maria gave her a big kiss.

John and the green dragon

John lay in bed asleep. He was dreaming of cars, motorbikes and flying into danger with Batman.

Downstairs his mother, father and two big brothers were busy in the family restaurant. The Hong Kong Chinese Restaurant stood in a row of shops in the high street of a small, country town. The neon light flashed on and off all day and night – 'TAKE AWAY . . . TAKE AWAY . . .' People did indeed come to take away a delicious, hot bag of Chinese food and rush home to eat it in front of the television. Other people liked to have a meal out just for a treat, and they would come into the restaurant and sit under the red-tasselled lanterns, leaning over the menu with watering mouths.

It was the night of the Chinese New Year. The swing doors flapped to and fro as steaming dishes were carried through to hungry people. Chicken with sliced almonds, green peppers and special fried rice at Table 26; shark fin soup followed by crispy duck and bamboo shoots at Table 11; spare ribs in black bean sauce, sweet and sour pork, bird's nest soup and beef chop suey all at Table 5 . . . the smells wafted upstairs, but John did not stir. Not so long ago he had had his favourite supper of egg, sausages, baked beans and chips.

Outside, the moon hung like a great lantern. Suddenly a shadow darkened the moonlit sky. John awoke. He could hear a rustling and whirling – like wind; a crackling and sparkling – like fire; a looping and swooping – like waves. Outside his window John saw a green head bobbing up and down – a dragon's head – with red, glowing eyes and a long, flaming tongue darting in and out between huge, spiky, white teeth. The dragon squeezed himself between the open windows. His jagged, green body and long, long tail came trailing inside and coiled itself around the room like a giant kite.

'Hello,' said John politely. 'Can I help you?'

'I've flown all the way from China,' said

the Green Dragon. 'Over snowy mountains
and icy lakes; winding rivers and smoking
factories; over vast fields of rice and wheat
– and now I am so hungry I could swallow
up your mother's kitchen.'

'Oh please don't do that,' cried John.
'My mother and father are very proud of
their kitchen. They say that we cook the best
Chinese food outside London. I help too
with sorting out the knives, forks and
spoons, and our customers call me Hong
Kong John.'

50

'Well then, Hong Kong John,' said the Green Dragon, 'since I am so hungry, and since it is the Chinese New Year, I think I should savour some of your famous food. After all – I am an expert. I have eaten at the finest tables in China – at feasts given by the great emperors themselves!'

'You must be very old if you have eaten with the emperors of China,' said John.

'Several hundred – maybe even a thousand,' boasted the dragon. 'Now then – about this food – I would like to eat deep fried pork with delectable seaweed; braised beef with soya sauce and noodles; bean curd with crab meat; king fried prawns with heavenly vegetables of the four seasons; but to start with I must sharpen my teeth on succulent spare ribs, and I'll finish with a bowl of lychees to sweeten me up. All this must be accompanied with a constant flow of hot, sweet-scented Jasmine tea – pots and pots of it. Well? What are you waiting for?' The Green Dragon looked at John impatiently.

'I . . . I can't get all *that*!' gasped John.

'Can't you?' The dragon looked downcast. He whisked his tail and ground his teeth. 'Well, what can you get me then?' he asked sulkily.

'I might be able to get you something from the set menus,' said John. 'You know – select a dish from A, B, C or D – and you get three courses all for three pounds.'

The Green Dragon heaved and rumbled. 'I don't care what you get me, anything, but get it fast before I start nibbling your curtains. I am absolutely starving!'

John crept downstairs. He peered through the bamboo screens at the bustling restaurant. His brothers looked like jugglers as they balanced plates and dishes piled high as pagodas, hurrying with orders from table to table. His father was mixing drinks at the bar, while his mother bent over sizzling saucepans in the kitchen behind. John tip-toed to the corner of the kitchen where they prepared the set menus. Taking one or two silver foil boxes he quickly scooped in some fried rice, chicken chop suey, a pancake roll, a few crispy balls of sweet and sour pork and a pineapple fritter. The dragon sucked everything into his mouth – boxes and all! 'Where is the tea . . . the tea . . . I must have some tea – I did tell you. . . '

'I really could not manage the tea,' said John, hoping that the dragon was not going to make trouble. 'I can get lemonade.' After gulping down several bottles of lemonade, the dragon licked his lips, stretched till it seemed he would push through the ceiling, then pointed his head towards the window. 'Are you ready to go?'

'Ready to go,' asked John, puzzled. 'Go where?'

'Why, to London of course,' said the dragon. 'I've come thousands of miles to see the New Year celebrations in . . . what is the name of that place . . . So . . . Ho . . .?'

'Soho!' cried John – 'but that's a hundred miles from here.'

'I came from China in only a moment or two, we'll be in London in a jiffy,' boasted the dragon. Filled with excitement, John clambered on to the dragon's back and snuggled between his great wings with his arms clasped around his neck. 'Which way?' asked the dragon as they rose high into the sky.

'We always go up the motorway,' replied John.

The motorway shone below them in the

moonlight like a winding silver ribbon. The cars and lorries flitted to and fro like dazzling insects. The next moment London lay below them – a million scattered lights. They swooped down over the river Thames and followed it up to Westminster. They turned left at Big Ben, up Pall Mall, past the Horse Guards, over Trafalgar Square and on up to Piccadilly. Suddenly a rocket sped up into the air showering them with sparks. 'I think we've arrived,' said the Green Dragon.

John could see a flutter of red flags and fairy lights garlanded across the street from roof-top to roof-top. Clashing cymbals and rattling drums filled the air. Laughing people danced about wearing strange masks, carrying streamers and gaily painted lanterns. A great paper lion wheeled in and out of the crowd, roaring and leaping as children chased and teased it.

'They must have known I was coming!' yelled the dragon. 'Look! They've hung the cabbages from their windows for me – I love cabbages.'

From almost every window, John could see Chinese cabbages dangling from the ends of string. For a moment the noise and frenzy of the crowd hushed in amazement as the Green Dragon came rushing in among them. Then there was a cheer of joy and everyone burst out laughing and shouting as the dragon zig-zagged from window to window gobbling up the cabbages. Children followed, pressing red-dyed melon seeds into John's hands and tossing red envelopes up to him with gifts inside. All around fireworks sprayed the sky and firecrackers spluttered at their feet.

'It's years since I saw a dragon dance,' murmured an elderly Chinese shopkeeper.

As the dance grew wilder, John's arms began to ache. He felt as if he were on a merry-go-round which would not stop. At last he could hold on no longer; his tired fingers loosened and he began to slide off the dragon's back. The dragon rollicked on through the crowd. John slithered to the ground, and before he could look around he was swept away by merry-makers and dancers. He tried to struggle after the Green Dragon, but gradually he found himself carried out of sight – down side streets and

55

up narrow alleys. Just as he was beginning to feel very lost, he felt a hand in his and turned to find a little girl at his side.

'You are the dragon boy, aren't you?' she said.

'Yes, but I've lost him,' said John sadly, 'and I can't get home without him.'

'Oh, don't worry,' replied the girl, 'he'll find you when it's time. What is your name?'

'John,' said John, 'but some people call me Hong Kong John. My Chinese name is Ying-Chai.'

'Ying-Chai!' the girl exclaimed. 'I like that for it means "Very Brave" and you must be brave to ride on a dragon's back. My name is Hoi-Au which means "Seagull". My English name is Marina.'

The children gaily jostled along the streets, chewing on melon seeds and dodging the firecrackers.

'I feel as if I were in China,' shouted John.

'Well, people do call this place "China Town" as there are many Chinese families living round here. Come and visit my house, we are nearly there.' They stopped outside a curio shop filled with Chinese statuettes

of jade and marble; paintings and orna-
ments; precious silks and manuscripts.

'This is my father's shop,' said Marina.
'We live upstairs above the shop.'

John followed Marina upstairs and
entered a room full of friendly people. They
all turned with smiling faces and out-
stretched hands of welcome to greet them.
Marina's mother came forward. 'Hello,
dragon boy, I am delighted to have you in
my home.' She bowed, then put a hand on
his shoulder and gently sat him down as
she could see that he was tired.

'His name is Ying-Chai,' Marina told
them. Then everyone gathered round him
and offered him Chinese sweets – salted,
dried apricots, sweet and sour bananas; and
there were bowls of prawn crackers and hot
tea or lemonade.

John met the rest of Marina's family.
'These are my two brothers and sister. We
are all at school in the neighbourhood. This
is my most respected eldest uncle, Mr Tsin.
He owns a restaurant just round the corner.
My most honoured grandfather is Mr
Leung and he owns a bookshop two streets
away.' John bowed deeply to Mr Tsin

and Mr Leung, and they bowed back to him.

'My family have a restaurant miles out of London in the country,' John contributed.

Everyone smiled. The night passed. A sudden swell of sound from the crowd sent everyone running to the window. John saw the Green Dragon being carried along by cheering merry-makers. As they drew near, the dragon called up to the window where John was leaning out anxiously, 'It's time to go home now, John!'

John turned to Marina and her family and wished them goodbye. 'Thank you for looking after me,' he said, 'and I hope you will visit me in the country, one day.'

The dragon hovered outside the window and John climbed out on to his back.

'Goodbye, John! Goodbye, Ying-Chai, brave dragon boy!' called his friends.

As the dragon turned westwards, the first glow of dawn was beginning to light up the horizon behind them. The last rocket spluttered to the ground, and the lanterns already looked dimmer by the new light of day. John saw no more. The dragon flew back down the motorway with the boy fast asleep between his wings. A few early morning workers, who happened to glance up at the sky, were amazed to see such a high-flying kite with its long, long tail trailing among the pink-streaked clouds.

The next morning John awoke to find his mother by his bed. 'Happy New Year, John,' she beamed. 'Welcome to the Year of the Dragon. Here is a parcel which has come all the way from your uncle in China.'

John carefully unwrapped the paper and uncovered a large, flat box. Hardly daring to breathe he lifted the lid. There lay a huge, green, paper kite shaped like a dragon, with red, glowing eyes, a long, flaming tongue between spiky, white teeth.

'I've flown all the way from China . . .' the dragon seemed to be saying, '. . . over snowy mountains and icy lakes; winding rivers and smoking factories . . . vast fields of rice and wheat . . . and . . .'

Midnight cows

Kath lived on the fifteenth floor of a high-rise block of flats. She could see the sky from every window. If she looked down from the balcony, the city looked like toy-land. Everything was so tiny. The cars looked no bigger than ladybirds and the people looked like ants! If she wanted to go out to play she had to wait for Mummy to find the time to take her. Then they would go to the lift and down fifteen floors to the bottom. If the lift was out of order they did not go at all.

Today it was raining and raining. Kath gazed out of the window at the heavy, grey clouds. They were going on holiday soon and she could hardly wait. Last year had been so hot. Days upon days of sunshine and cotton frocks. Even the nights had been hot and she only slept under a sheet.

They always went to Ireland for their holidays. Her Uncle Patrick had a farm where the pastures ran down to the sea. He had a herd of dairy cows. They were soft, fat, creamy cows with dark brown blotches, and whisky tails to flick away the flies. When Dad and Uncle Patrick, his brother, were children, they would be up at the crack of dawn to milk the cows by hand – just as they do in nursery rhymes – sitting on a stool with a pail to catch the milk. Now Uncle Patrick had a milking machine. It was so much quicker because he could do nearly all the cows at once.

Kath loved to go into the cow sheds at milking time. She knew all the cows by name: Philomel, Clarabel, Annabel, Lou Loubel; and Annette, Elspeth, Susette and Bernadette . . . and lots more.

After milking, Kath would help her uncle to herd the cows out into the farmyard. Then she would open the gate and they would ramble out into the road and down to their rich, green grazing fields by the sea. There they spent their day munching and munching, while the sea came in and the sea went out. In the evening all the cows would turn their heads towards the sun and wait for the farmer to come and take them home.

Now as she stared at the dreary rain, Kath remembered one summer night last year in Ireland when she could not sleep. It was too warm. Her window was open to catch every breeze, but even the sea sounded lazy. It slurped against the shore as if turned to syrup. She heard the cows mooing and kicking their stalls. They were restless too.

'I know what the cows need,' thought Kath to herself. 'They need a nice cool walk along the shore.'

She jumped quietly out of bed, tiptoed downstairs and out into the yard. The moon was full and gave plenty of light. She opened the cow-shed door and went to each stall calling softly . . . 'Philomel . . . Clarabel . . . Annabel . . . Susette . . . Bernadette . . . come on! Let's go down to the sea and get cool.' The cows turned their heads and looked at her with huge, brown eyes.

'What a good idea,' they seemed to say.

One by one they sauntered out into the yard. Kath opened the gate and led them down the road to the sea.

A distant church clock struck twelve. The moon sparkled and danced on the sea as Kath and the midnight cows meandered along the shore, stepping in and out of the waves.

Suddenly, she smelt something delicious! The aroma of fish roasting over a fire. As she rounded a large rock, she saw a small fishing boat, and near by up the shingle was a group of gypsies. They had made a fire out of driftwood and were cooking their supper.

When they saw Kath they jumped with surprise. 'Are you a fairy?' they asked. She looked a bit like a fairy as she was only wearing her frilly nightdress.

'Oh no!' she laughed, 'I'm only Kathleen Moriarty. The cows and I were too hot to sleep, so I brought them down to the shore to get cool.'

'We've been fishing,' said the gypsies, 'and caught some mackerel. Would you care for a bite to eat?'

Kath's mouth watered. 'Yes please,' she said.

While Kath ate the mackerel, the gypsies sang songs, and the cows wandered across the beach munching rock flowers and sand grass.

'If you have a bucket,' Kath said, 'I'm sure I could give you some milk. I learned to milk by hand when there was a power cut once and we couldn't use our milking machine. Our cows give plenty, and we always have some to spare.'

The gypsies looked pleased. 'Our caravan is just up there,' said one. 'I'll go and get a bucket.' When he came back, Kath called Philomel. Philomel stood quietly while Kath placed the bucket underneath her udders. Then, sitting on a rock, Kath pressed her cheek against the cow's warm, soft body, and with gentle tugging movements began to milk her. The pure, white milk spurted into the bucket, and soon there was plenty to go round.

Kath began to feel sleepy. Some of the cows were moving up the beach into the pasture, ready to go home.

'Thank you for the mackerel,' said Kath.

'Thank you for the milk,' they replied. Then, because she was too tired to walk, the gypsies lifted Kath on to Philomel's back.

The cows did not need Kath to show them the way home. Slowly and silently they ambled back across the fields and up the road. They filed through the open farm gate and into their stalls. Kath had fallen fast asleep on Philomel's back. She did not

awake even when she slid gently into the straw lining the stall. There she slept for the rest of the night, as down on the shore the gypsies sang round their fire until dawn. They drank the sweet milk and wondered if they would ever see Kath and her midnight cows again.

The rain fell like a curtain. As Kath looked over the wet, misty city, a silvery sun brightened the wide, grey sky. The sky looked like the sea, and Kath couldn't wait to go back to Ireland. 'Would the gypsies be there again this year?' she wondered.

Mummy came in. 'Rain or no rain, we must go shopping,' she said. Kath put on her raincoat and boots and went out happily to the lift.

The miraculous orange tree

Joey lived in a house in the middle of a large city. There was a small space at the back of Joey's house which could not rightly be called a garden as there was no lawn and no flower-beds. The space was all covered over in concrete and they called it the backyard. It was quite good for playing ball or riding a bicycle round and round when the weather was dry; but when it rained, Joey would watch the raindrops bouncing on the grey stone and he wondered if he would ever see the place he had heard his mother and father talk about. They had seen a place which was always sunny – where there was plenty of space, sea – and orange trees! There were few trees where Joey lived – apart from those in the park – and he could hardly imagine what an orange tree looked like.

One morning Joey woke early. It was summer and the sun was shining. From his bed, Joey could see a chink of bright, blue sky through the curtains. He jumped up and ran to look out of the window. As he drew the curtains – what a sight met his eyes! There standing in the middle of the backyard was – an Orange Tree!

Joey thought he must still be asleep. He turned his back, shut his eyes and counted to ten; then he looked again. It was still there. An Orange Tree. There was no doubt about it, for it was laden with oranges.

Joey ran to his parents' room. His mother and father were still asleep

'Ma! Pa!' cried Joey.

'Go away, we're still sleeping,' groaned Pa.

'There's an Orange Tree in our backyard,' said Joey, shaking his Ma.

'It's another of your dreams, Joey, now go away and don't be a nuisance.'

Joey ran to the window. Yes it was still there.

'I'm not dreaming, Ma, I can see it from your window too – oh please come and look!' begged Joey.

Pa snorted and pulled the bedclothes over his ears. Ma sighed, 'Joey, now don't go and get your Pa and me all mad. Go away and play.'

She rolled over and pulled the bedclothes up over her ears.

Joey's grandfather lived with them. So Joey ran to him.

'Grandfather, Grandfather! Have you seen the Orange Tree in our backyard?'

'Are you making up stories again, Joey?' asked Grandfather sternly.

Joey begged his grandfather just to look out of the window.

'If I'm telling stories, you can whack me with your slipper.'

So Grandfather looked out of the window.

Joey held his breath. Was the Orange Tree still there? He closed his eyes.

'Suffering Catfish!' whispered Grandfather. (He always said that when he was surprised.)

Joey and Grandfather stood in silence for a long time gazing at the Orange Tree. At last Grandfather said, 'Well, I guess we'd better tell your Pa.'

'He'll never believe you,' said Joey. 'I've tried.'

'He'll believe me,' said Grandfather firmly.

Joey's mother and father were still lying

in bed with the bedclothes pulled over their ears when Joey and his grandfather entered the room. Grandfather nudged Joey to speak first.

'Ma! Pa! I wish to inform you that there is an Orange Tree in our backyard.'

The two humps under the bedclothes didn't stir.

'Did you hear what Joey said?' bellowed Grandfather – with such a roar that Joey's Ma and Pa sat bolt upright like jack-in the-boxes.

'There is an Orange Tree in the back-yard.'

Ma and Pa got out of bed and went to the window.

'*Suffering catfish!*' they gasped with astonishment. 'There *is* an Orange Tree.'

'What do we do now, Grandfather?' asked Joey.

'What do we do? Why, we pick as many oranges as we can and then ask all our neighbours in for a party!'

So they all got dressed and rushed out into the backyard with poles and baskets and a ladder and began to pick the oranges.

Soon they had several baskets full. Then Joey's ma put on her best Sunday hat and went round to all the neighbours inviting them to a party.

Everyone agreed that it was the best party in years. The boys got out their guitars and drums, and everyone danced and sang long into the evening. As for the oranges, they got eaten up with the speed of lightning.

'Oh my, I haven't tasted oranges like this since I was a boy,' said Grandfather dreamily, sucking his fifth orange.

'It's just like home,' said one old lady.

'Where did you get them?' asked another.

'We got a tree,' said Ma.

'Ha ha ha ha ha . . .' the guests roared with laughter.

'My, oh my, an orange tree did you say . . . in your backyard? Ha ha ha ha.'

Soon the whole party was rocking with laughter.

Ma ran to the window and pulled back the curtain. 'See for yourselves,' she said.

Outside it was night. The sky was starry and bright with a new moon. The backyard was empty. The Orange Tree had gone. Everyone ran outside.

'Look!' cried Joey, collecting some sprigs of fallen leaves.

'This proves the tree was here.'

Everyone stopped laughing. They looked at the leaves and sniffed the air which was rich with the smell of oranges. Somehow they all knew that it was true. Amazed, they thanked Joey, his ma, pa and his grandfather for the party, and went home to talk about the miraculous Orange Tree.

Joey pressed the orange leaves in a book. Whenever it was a dull, grey, rainy day, he would open the book and a faint smell of oranges would float upwards and remind him of that summer, when for one day an Orange Tree had stood in his own backyard.

Anna in the land of clocks

Anna loved visiting her Polish aunt. Apart from her delicious Polish teas with Baba cakes and Piernik – Hurry Guests Are Coming – Biscuits, she loved her house. From the outside her house was a semi-detached in a row of others all exactly the same, but inside, Aunt Josepha's home brimmed over with interesting things. The walls were dotted with paintings, the wooden floors were strewn with gaily coloured carpets; the grand piano was crowded with old brown photographs and the bay window was a jungle of potted plants.

But what Anna liked best of all in Aunt Josepha's house was the great, big grandfather clock standing in the hall. What a story there was about that grandfather clock! When Aunt Josepha and Uncle Andrzej were escaping from the war in Poland, Uncle Andrzej refused to leave behind the great clock. His grandfather had made it and passed it on to his father. So

Uncle Andrzej said he could not allow it to fall into anyone else's hands. He stuffed it full of what precious family belongings he could; strapped it to a trolley and trundled it across Europe to England.

It was made from dark brown, polished wood with deep carvings decorating its front. The face of the clock was mysterious; a painted moon with a strange sad face looked down from one side and a jolly laughing sun beamed down from the other. The numbers paraded round the face – bold and black – and the hands pointed out the time with long elegant fingers.

Most of all, Anna liked to watch the silver pendulum swinging to and fro . . . to and fro . . . tick . . . tock . . . tick . . . tock . . . Then whenever the hands reached the hour, like three o'clock, there would be a peculiar whirring and clicking and then – dong . . . dong . . . dong . . . the clock would strike with commanding notes.

One day Anna was playing near the clock when suddenly the clock went tick . . . tock . . . tick . . . and nothing! The clock had stopped. Anna looked at the pendulum. It was hanging down quite still.

'I've never known the clock to stop before,' she thought. 'I wonder what the matter is.' She gave the side a couple of gentle taps. Tap! Tap!

'Come in!' croaked the strangest, squeakiest voice Anna had ever heard. She stepped back in amazement. The door opened and from behind the pendulum leaned the oddest, crinkliest, tiniest little man that Anna had ever seen.

'Come in! Come in!' beckoned the old man. 'You knocked, didn't you?'

'I thought I tapped,' said Anna. 'The clock has stopped.'

'Of course it has,' said the old man. 'I stopped it. I am the Grand Master of the Clocks. Now do you want to come in or don't you? I have a lot to do before the Royal Inspection today.'

'It's nearly tea-time,' replied Anna doubtfully, 'and Aunt Josepha has invited the Petrowskis to tea.'

'There's plenty of time!' croaked the old man, 'and I could do with your help. Come in, come in!' He reached out and helped Anna into the clock. Somewhere in the musty darkness they pushed through

76

another door behind the pendulum and out they stepped into the Land of Clocks!

Anna had never seen so many clocks. There were tall clocks, oval clocks, small clocks, fat clocks, travelling clocks, hanging clocks, sitting clocks and ever such fancy clocks – and they all ticked in a hundred ways.

Deep slow ticking . . . TICK . . . TOCK . . . TICK . . . TOCK . . .

High fast ticking . . . tick tick tick tick.

No stuff and nonsense ticking . . . tick . . . tock . . . tick . . . tock . . .

Rhythmic ticking . . . tickety . . . tockety . . . tickety . . . tockety . . .

Suddenly there was a churning and a whirring, a clicking and a spinning of wheels.

'Good! The clocks are about to strike,' said the Grand Master.

It was like the sound of an orchestra as they all began together.

DONG . . . DONG . . . DONG . . .

Ting . . . ting . . . ting . . . ting . . .

Chime . . . chime . . . chime . . .

Cuckoo . . . cuckoo . . . cuckoo . . .

Little figures sprang out of doors that

opened and closed. Dancers twirled, birds flew and rabbits hopped.

'It's wonderful!' cried Anna.

'Mustn't dawdle. Mustn't dawdle!' muttered the old man. 'Here, girl! Take this

cloth and polish the clocks for me whilst I see to their insides.'

At last all the delicate springs were oiled and the cogs were spinning. Every clock had been wound up from one of a hundred keys hanging from the old man's waist. Every clock had been set, polished and dusted.

'Hurry now – we barely have time to

arrange the Clocks of Honour,' panted the Grand Master. Anna helped him to position a row of tall, smart, gleaming clocks into a Guard of Honour. They made sure all the other clocks were lined up ready for the Royal Inspection which was about to begin.

Just then all the wheels and cogs began to spin and click. 'It's time!' hissed the old man, 'stand to attention.'

As the whole Land of Clocks struck a fanfare – the King appeared, the tallest, grandest most magnificent of clocks – and on time.

'Good gracious! It's Aunt Josepha's grandfather clock,' gasped Anna.

'Oh dear! I do hope that everything is perfect,' whispered the Grand Master, 'the King is very particular.'

The King moved from clock to clock . . . examining and listening. . . . Suddenly he reached Anna. He examined. He listened. He frowned.

'Grand Master,' he thundered. 'Here is a clock which does not tick.'

'I'm not a clock, I'm a girl,' Anna protested. 'Anyway, if you put your ear to my chest you will find that I do tick. I just don't tell the time.'

The King put his ear to Anna's chest. Her heart was beating steadily if a little fast.

'Remarkable!' said the King. But he still looked puzzled. 'It is not a clock but a girl. It ticks but does not tell the time. Remarkable!'

The inspection was over. The clocks struck up a *Grande Polonaise* and swept into a dance. They whirled about sparkling and flashing until Anna's eyes were quite bedazzled and her eyes began to close. 'Oh dear, I'm falling asleep. How rude of me,' she thought as she slid to the ground, leaning against the King.

'Wake up, Anna! Wake up!' Aunt Josepha was gently shaking Anna. She opened her eyes.

'I think that old grandfather clock put you to sleep. You had your ear against his side. Now hurry up and wash. It's tea-time and the Petrowskis will be here in a minute. I've made your favourite Babki and custard!'

Anna looked at the grandfather clock and

bowed. 'It's tea-time, your majesty,' she whispered and bowed very low.

DONG . . . DONG . . . DONG . . . DONG . . . replied the King.

Danny and the cats

It was the sound of a cat that awoke Danny
from his sleep. A cat wailing, squawling,
miaowing and caterwauling. Although it was
the middle of the night, it was as light as
day. Danny jumped out of bed and looked
out of the window. A huge moon glowed in
the sky. He could see right to the end of the
street – as far as the church.

The church was not used as a church any
more, but it was Danny's playground.
Although the gates were locked he knew a
railing that was bent where he could squeeze
inside. He liked to run up the stone steps
to the great oak door, then slide down the
iron railing. He knew the narrow alley
which ran all round the church. Tentacles
of blackberry bushes straggled fiercely
down the walls waiting to tear his shirt as
he ran by. But who cared? The blackberries
tasted delicious! Once he had found a side
door that opened when he pushed. Danny
had gone inside, his heart thumping. Even

82

his breath seemed to echo as he tiptoed down the aisle. Then a cat jumped out, and Danny fled as if chased by a ghost.

Danny stood now staring down at the church. Through the railings he could make out a circle of cats. They were sitting in the forecourt and seemed to be holding a meeting. 'Perhaps they are having a union meeting like the ones Dad goes to,' thought Danny with a grin.

Suddenly he heard a low moan close by. It was Winnie, the Hortons' cat from next door. She sprang up the basement steps and on to a wall. She paused for a moment, her tail waving stiffly like a stick. Danny could see her yellow eyes gleaming as bright as headlamps. She moaned softly then leapt down on to the pavement and padded off towards the church. From out of the shadows flitted another cat. It was Spicer from No. 23. Then he saw another and another – all hurrying to the church.

Danny longed to know what was going on. He pulled on his plimsolls and a pullover on top of his pyjamas. He crept down the hall to the kitchen, then stood for a moment listening. Danny's father was a milkman.

His clean, white coat and peaked cap hung on the door. His mum had laid the table ready for an early breakfast. The house breathed; he could hear his father's gentle snores coming from the bedroom; the clock ticking away on the old Welsh dresser; and the fridge throbbing rhythmically in the corner. Danny quietly opened the kitchen door and put it on the latch. Then he slipped out into the night.

The cool air made him gasp. He felt excited, tingly, almost as if he were a cat too. He slunk down the side of the house and dashed across the street. As he came nearer and nearer to the church, he could hear the cats moaning and growling as they talked to each other in their strange cat language. Danny found his bent railing and squeezed in. 'Yowl! Miaow! Prrriaow!' Danny had never seen so many cats. Some he recognised, like Winnie and Spicer, but there were very many others he did not know. One cat seemed to be their leader. He was the biggest and shaggiest. When Danny looked at him he shuddered. He was an ancient, fierce, battle-worn tabby; one ear was almost completely chewed off, and he had only half a tail; worst of all was a scar which ran from an eye-brow right down to his nose. He looked like a cat who had lived at least eight of his nine lives.

Danny was sure that he had made no sound – that he had barely breathed, but all of a sudden he knew that they knew he was there. A forest of burning eyes turned on him. He was transfixed. Then one cat broke away from the others and padded towards him. It was Winnie! Danny gave a gasp of relief. Surely Winnie was his friend. She was always round at his back door begging for titbits – and getting them. To his amazement, Winnie spoke – or did she? All Danny knew was that he understood. She said, 'Hullo, Danny! What are you doing here?'

'You woke me up,' said Danny, 'and I wanted to come and see what was happening.'

'That was very inquisitive of you,' said Winnie crossly.

'Yes, I suppose it was, but you were making such a din that it's a wonder you did not waken the whole street,' replied Danny.

'Yowl! Miaow!' There came a terrible cry. It was the leader, Scarface.

'Who is that human being? Send him away!'

'It's Danny Evans, the milkman's boy,' said Winnie.

'The milkman's boy?' A great purr broke out like a throbbing engine. Danny felt the atmosphere change; there was a sound of licking and smacking of lips.

'Danny Evans,' crooned Scarface. 'A good Welsh name.' Scarface looked wonderfully pleased. Two years ago he had been left behind in Wales when his family had

moved down south looking for work. He had tried to follow them, but after days and weeks of trailing forlornly down the motorway, he had landed up here. His experiences so impressed the neighbourhood cats that they had welcomed him as a leader.

'You may stay, Danny Evans bach, and be our honoured guest!' said Scarface grandly.

So Danny joined the circle of cats and sat cross-legged next to Winnie.

'We meet like this every full moon,' whispered Winnie. 'We discuss all our problems – mainly food! A lot of us have our human families who feed and shelter us, but others are strays and have to pick up what they can. We don't like to see starving cats in our neighbourhood. It gives us a bad image. So we formed this union to make sure that every cat has a fair deal.'

'Parker!' Scarface was addressing a rather mangy cat. 'Have you found yourself a regular supply of food yet?'

Parker stood up and twirled his tail. 'Yes!' he purred. 'The new family at No. 21 are leaving titbits for me. The children like me, and if I'm lucky they may even take me in!'

'Whisky! What about you?'

Whisky was a marmalade cat. 'I'm not starving,' she said sulkily, 'but the food is not exactly what I would have chosen. I dare say I'll get used to it – it's a case of having to.'

'What do you mean?' asked Scarface impatiently. 'What kind of food?'

'Curry!' hissed the marmalade cat. 'The Singhs at No. 45 leave me dahl and chapattis and vindaloo!'

If cats could giggle, that is how Danny would have described the sound of sniffling and snuffling that broke out.

'It's all right for you to laugh,' said Whisky, 'but I nearly threw myself into the canal the first time I ate curry!'

'You will get used to it,' said a black and white cat. 'I got used to spaghetti bolognese and pizza from the Italian restaurant.'

'My people are vegetarian,' said another, 'so I had to get used to cheese and spinach flans.'

Scarface called the meeting to order.

'Now, before we discuss who has the left-overs at the fish and chip shop this week, are there any other problems?'

'Yes, I have a problem,' called out a sleek little grey cat called Selena. 'I get my food from Mr Biggs at No. 19. But for the past week he has left me nothing – not even a bacon rind.' There was a murmur of sympathy. 'I think he may be ill. He didn't take in his bottle of milk today.'

'That sounds like a job for my dad and me,' interrupted Danny.

Dozens of burning eyes turned once again on Danny. 'If Mr Biggs has milk, then I expect my dad delivers it to him. He always keeps a lookout for uncollected bottles of milk. I can find out if Mr Biggs is ill.' The cats listened. They did not twitch even the tip of a tail. Somewhere a clock was striking. Danny felt tired. The cats said they would be grateful for his help. Danny said he must go to bed now if he was to be up in time to go on the rounds with his dad. So he said 'Goodnight' to the cats and slipped back through the railings.

Danny slept deeply and dreamed. He

dreamed he was a cat sneaking in and out of the church; running nimbly along the tops of walls and fences and prowling secretly down dark alleys.

The alarm clock broke into his dreams – at first shrilly – then muffled as his dad stuffed it under his pillow. Danny awoke slowly. He could hear his father getting up and singing as he went. He was very good at singing 'Land of our Fathers' and brushing his teeth at the same time. He often sang a solo in chapel on Sundays.

'Can I come with you today?' asked Danny.

'Awake already, are you, Danny bach?' said Dad. 'Yes, you can come if it's all right with your mam.'

It was all right. After breakfast, Dad got out his bicycle. He always biked to the depot where he would collect his milk float. Danny sat astride on the back while Dad cycled down the silent, grey streets. Danny climbed up on to the milk float next to his dad. It was stacked high with ice-cold milk. Danny loved helping his dad on the round. Many a morning he had hummed up and down the streets helping to deliver the milk and collect the empties. Sometimes there was money to pick up wrapped in an envelope and hidden under a bottle; or there were the messages tucked inside necks of bottles – like 'Please leave an extra pint'; or, 'No milk today thank you.'

He never went in the winter. Mum drew the line at that. Dad had to go to work in the pitch dark. It was freezing, and he bundled up in winter woollies under his coat. Mum had knitted him special gloves with the finger-tips out, so that he could grip the bottles safely. But as soon as the mornings got lighter, Danny was allowed to go with his dad. The best thing he liked was that he and Dad were the only people up in the whole town. They hardly saw anyone first thing – except a few early morning workers rushing down the High Street for the first bus. The houses slept behind drawn curtains – and not even a cat crossed their path. Danny wondered if his meeting with the cats last night had all been a dream. He would soon know. They arrived at No. 19 where old Mr Biggs lived. He took a pint and went down the basement steps to his door. It had not been a dream. Selena, the grey and white cat, was right. There was the bottle of milk standing uncollected.

'Hey, Dad,' he called, 'Mr Biggs hasn't taken his pint from yesterday.' His dad came to see and knocked on the door.

No one answered. He knocked again and called out. 'Mr Biggs! Are you home?' Suddenly they heard a faint groan. His dad pushed the kitchen door and it opened. In a back room they found Mr Biggs lying in bed. 'Oh I'm so glad you've found me,' he said weakly, 'I don't feel at all well.'

His dad went off to phone for a doctor, while Danny stayed with the old man. 'What a good thing you and your dad took the trouble to call,' he said.

A grey and white face appeared at the window. It was Selena. 'That cat is a stray, but she's attached herself to me. I never have very much to give her – just bacon rind and a saucer of milk – but she always comes. She seemed to be the only one who knew I was ill. Could you give her a saucer of milk, Danny?' Danny carefully placed a saucer of milk outside the kitchen door. Selena jumped down, purring. Just before she dipped her mouth down to drink, she looked at Danny and said, 'Prrriaow, thank you!'

At the next full moon, Danny stood at his window. He stared down at the church, the church where he played and where the cats held their meetings. Sleek shapes moved in the shadows, and a low moaning sounded like the wind. Winnie sprang up the basement steps; Spicer flitted from fence to fence; cats were converging on the church from every direction. Whose turn would it be to get the fish and chip shop leftovers this time?

Danny pulled on his plimsolls and his pullover on top of his pyjamas. He tiptoed down the hall to the kitchen; past the table all set for breakfast. He opened the kitchen door, put it on the latch and slipped out into the night.